Parker Penguin and the WINTER GAMES

by Jon Chardiet • Illustrated by Charles Micucci

To Holt — J.C.

To Kathy and Danny — C.M.

Library of Congress Cataloging-in-Publication Data

Chardiet, Jon.
Parker Penguin and the Winter Games / by Jon Chardiet; illustrated by Charles Micucci.
p. cm.—(Read with me)
"Cartwheel Books."
Summary: Even though his team is the worst in the school, Parker Penguin cares only about winning the Winter Games, until his father shows him that winnng isn't everything.
ISBN 0-590-14925-3
[1. Winning and losing—Fiction. 2. Winter sports—Fiction. 3. Penguins—Fiction. 4. Animals—Fiction.] I. Micucci, Charles, ill. II. Title.
III. Series: Read with me (New York, N.Y.).
PZ7.C37365Par 1999
[E]—dc21

98-27869
CIP
AC

10 9 8 7 6 5 4 3 2 1 9/9 0/0 01 02 03 04

Printed in the U.S.A. 24
First printing, January 1999

On the first day of winter, Mr. Owly made an exciting announcement.

"It's almost time for the Winter Games," he said. "There will be hockey, cross-country skiing, and a toboggan race."

Everyone in the class started cheering. . . except Parker Penguin.

On the way home, the gang was talking about the Winter Games.

"Since Parker is the best athlete, I think he should be the captain of our team!" said Sally Seal.

"All right!" everyone shouted.
But Parker didn't say anything.

"What's wrong, Parker?" asked Rita Snow Rabbit.

"Every time we play against Mrs. Walrus's class, we get creamed!" said Parker. "I can see it now. First, Wanda Wolf will trash us in the toboggan race. Then, Morty Moose will crush us in the cross-country ski race. . . and if that's not enough, the Bear Brothers will bury us in hockey!"

"That's not good team spirit!" said Lester Lemming.
"Ha!" said Parker. "This isn't a team! It's a joke!"
"Hey, that's not nice!" said Sally Seal.
Parker just turned and walked away.

Parker walked all the way home by himself.

That night at dinner, Parker couldn't eat.
"What's wrong?" asked Papa Penguin.
Parker told his dad the whole story.
"I want to show you something," said Papa Penguin.

"Here's a picture of me on the hockey team," said Papa Penguin. "I had some of the best times of my life playing on this team."

Parker was curious. "Did you win any prizes or championships?" he asked.

"No," said Papa Penguin, "but I had a lot of fun. Sometimes that's more important than winning."

"Nothing is more important than winning," said Parker.

The next day after school, Mr. Owly blew a whistle.
"Okay, class," he said. "It's time to practice!"
First they practiced cross-country skiing.
Billy Bear fell on top of Lester
Lemming.

Fred Snow Fox knocked Mr. Owly into a snow drift.

And Rita Snow Rabbit got so excited, she started hopping and hopped right into a tree — skis and all.

Then they climbed a big hill and got ready to practice for the toboggan race.

"On your mark, get set — GO!" said Mr. Owly.

Rita Snow Rabbit covered her eyes.

Billy Bear squeezed Sally Seal so hard, she fell out of the toboggan.

Soon they were spinning out of control. *BAM!*

They crashed into a big woodpile.

Finally, it was time to practice hockey.
First, Fred Snow Fox crashed into Billy Bear!
Then, Sally Seal got hungry and cut a hole in the ice
and started fishing!

Meanwhile, Rita Snow Rabbit got so excited, she started hopping. She broke the ice and plunged into the pond — skates and all!

Everyone laughed — except Parker. “This team is a joke!” he cried. “We’ll *never* win the Winter Games!”

Just then, Wanda Wolf, Morty Moose, and the Bear Brothers came over.

"Hey, Captain Penguin!" said Morty Moose. "Ready to get creamed tomorrow?"

"You're the only one who's going to get creamed tomorrow," said Parker.

"HA!" laughed Morty Moose. "We'll see about that!" And then they walked away.

"Oh no," said Parker. "What are we going to do?"

Even Mr. Owly looked sad.

"Ready for the games?" asked Papa Penguin that night after supper.

"NO!" said Parker. "We're going to lose everything so badly that everyone will laugh at us!"

Papa Penguin thought for a while before he spoke.

"Grab your stick and skates!" he said.

"Where are we going?" asked Parker.

"To play *hockey*!" said Papa Penguin.

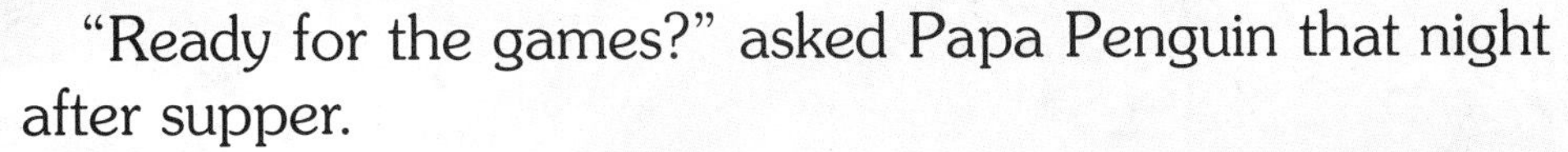

They went to the old pond and
played and played in the moonlight
for what seemed like hours.

When they were finished, they went to the Igloo Diner and had hot chocolate and pumpkin pie.

"That was fun!" said Parker Penguin.

"Yes," said Papa Penguin. "And how many games did you win?"

"I can't remember!" Parker said.

"That's because it's fun to play whether you win or not," Papa Penguin said.

The next morning, Parker got up extra early. He took scissors, some magic markers, and an old sheet his mother gave him.

"What are you doing?" asked Papa Penguin before he left for work.

"It's a secret!" said Parker.

Meanwhile, the whole school was lined up on the big hill for the toboggan race.

"Where's Parker?" asked Lester Lemming.

"It doesn't matter!" said Sally Seal. "We're going to get creamed with him or without him."

Just then they heard a noise.

"What's that?" asked Fred Snow Fox.

It was Parker! He was marching up the hill carrying a flag and blowing a bugle!

"Hooray!" said Parker when he got to the top of the hill.

"Three cheers for Mr. Owly's class — the best class in the school! Rah, rah, sis boom bah!"

Parker marched up to Mr. Owly and saluted. "Captain Penguin reporting for duty!" he said. Then he turned to the gang.

"Are you ready to go, guys?" he asked.

"YAAAYYY!" everybody shouted.

The Games began.

"Get ready. . . Get set. . . GO!" cried Mr. Owly.

The two toboggans raced down the hill.

"Oh no!" cried Lester Lemming. "We're going the wrong way!"

They were heading straight for the ski jump.

"AIEEE!" they cried as they flew through the air.

BAM! Mr. Owly's team crashed into a snowman!
"That's it!" said Fred Snow Fox. "We're going to come in last."
"Don't worry," said Parker. "We still have two events to go."

Then it was time for the cross-country ski race. All the skiers went up to the starting line to wait for Mr. Owly's signal.

"Go, Rita Snow Rabbit! Go!" Parker and the gang cried.

"Get ready to be creamed!" said Morty Moose.

But Rita got so excited, she started hopping up and down in place! All the other racers thought it looked like fun, so they started hopping, too.

"Ready. . . Set. . . GO!" Mr. Owly cried.

But everyone kept hopping up and down — except for Morty Moose, who won the race easily.

"We're never gonna win now!" said Sally Seal.

"Don't worry!" said Parker. "There's still one more event."

It was time for the big hockey game. The Bear Brothers easily scored a lot of goals early in the game.

For the first time, Parker wasn't worried about losing. He was having fun, and he played better than he ever had.

By the end of the game, the two teams were tied.

With ten seconds to go, Lester Lemming skated right between the Bear Brothers' legs and passed the puck to Parker, who knocked it in for a goal.

"YAAY!" everyone shouted. "We won!"

At the school assembly, the principal announced the winners of the Winter Games.

"First place, Mrs. Walrus's class!" said the principal.

"And in second place, Mr. Owly's class!"

Everybody cheered!

"We still creamed you!" said Morty Moose.

"Maybe so," said Parker Penguin. "But *we* had fun — and there's always next year!"